D0688926

231.765
Spirin, Gennadii.
Creation.
c2008.

1/09

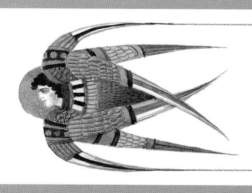

GENNADY SPIRIN

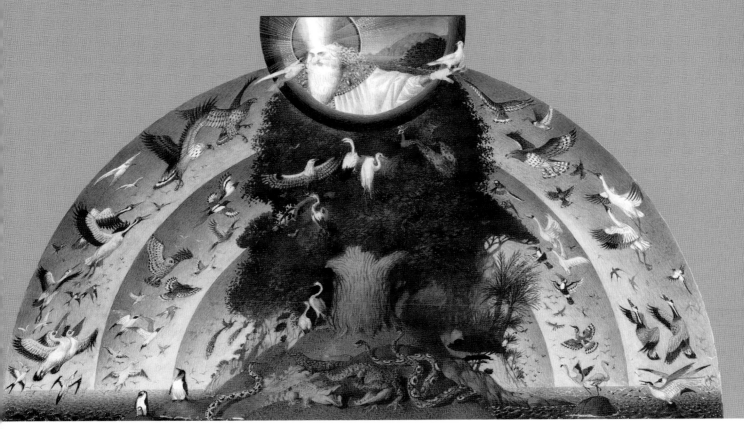

CREATION

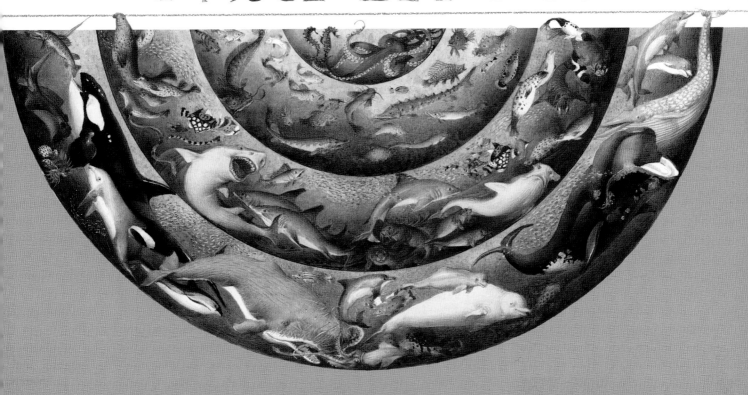

ZONDERVAN®

Creation
Copyright © 2008 by Zondervan
Illustrations © 2008 by Gennady Spirin

Requests for information should be addressed to: Grand Rapids, Michigan 49530

Library of Congress Cataloging-in-Publication Data

Spirin, Gennadii.
Creation / illustrated by Gennady Spirin.
p. cm. – (Master illustrator series)
ISBN-13: 978-0-310-71084-4 (hardcover)
ISBN-10: 0-310-71084-7 (hardcover)
1. Creation–Juvenile literature. I. Title. II. Title: Creation.
BS651.S75 2006
231.7′65–dc22
2006027617

All Scripture quotations unless otherwise noted are taken from the *Holy Bible: New International Version*®. NIV®.
Copyright © 1973, 1978, 1984 by International Bible Society. Used by permission of Zondervan. All rights reserved.

All rights reserved. No part of this publication may be reproduced, stored in a retrieval system, or transmitted in any form or
by any means—electronic, mechanical, photocopy, recording, or any other—except for brief quotations in printed reviews,
without the prior permission of the publisher.

Design: Laura Maitner-Mason

Illustrations used in this book were created using watercolors with paintbrush.
The body text for this book is set in Oneleigh Regular.

Printed in China

08 09 10 11 12 •10 9 8 7 6 5 4 3 2 1

The Bible says God created man based in his own likeness. I feel that this gives the artist the right to represent the image of the Creator based on his or her own interpretation. When I review the history of art and the artists who have tried to illustrate God's image, I find that the interpretations are unique and individual. Naturally, artists represent God according to their beliefs about how he should appear.

But there is one theme that unites all of these representations—a great love for the Creator. Love is the key element and inspiration of the work, and this love unites the Creator with his creation.

Everything that God creates, he creates with love: the grass, the flowers, the trees, the animals, the birds, and his greatest creation—people—bestowing upon us his own likeness. Likeness does not only mean our appearance. God gave humans a great gift: the ability to create—a godly ability. And we co-create with God during our lives on earth.

I cannot imagine a more valuable gift, and my tremendous gratitude fills me with joy and love towards our Creator.

Praise the Lord our Father,
God's Servant,

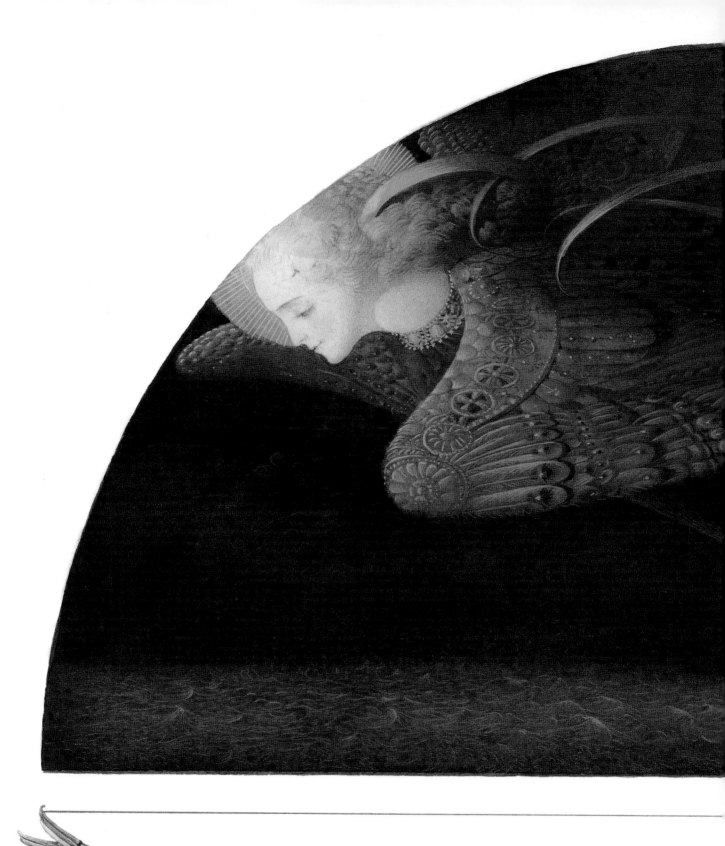

In the beginning God created the heavens and the earth.

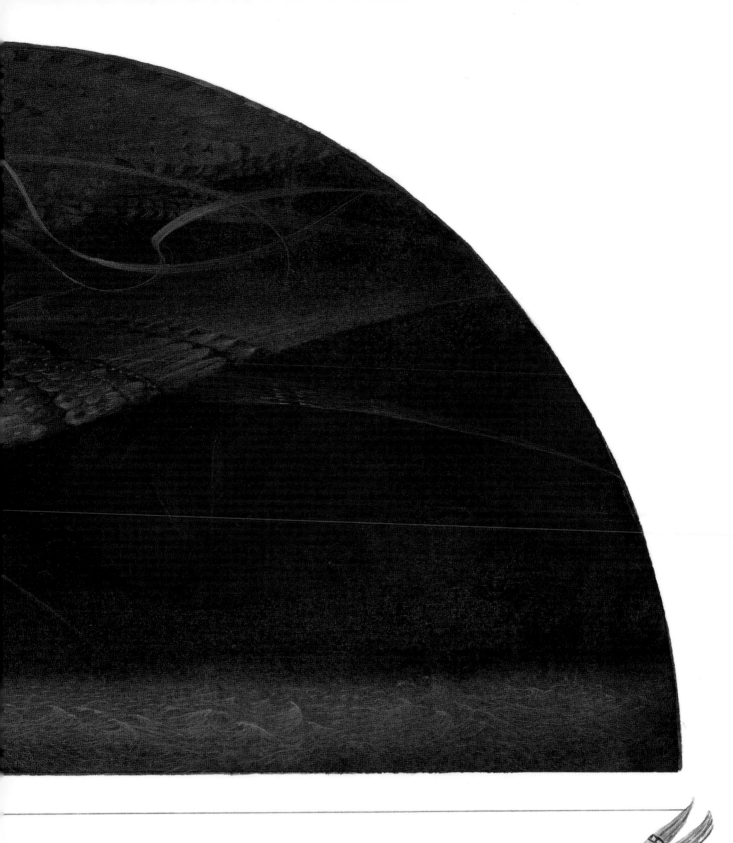

Now the earth was formless and empty, darkness was over the
surface of the deep, and the Spirit of God was hovering over the waters.
And God said, "Let there be light," and there was light.

God saw that the light was good, and he
separated the light from the darkness.
God called the light "day," and the darkness
he called "night." And there was evening,
and there was morning—the first day.

And God said,
"Let there be an expanse between the
waters to separate water from water."
So God made the expanse and separated the water under
the expanse from the water above it. And it was so.

God called the expanse "sky."
And there was evening, and there was morning—the second day.

And God said,
"Let the water under the sky be gathered to one place,
and let dry ground appear." And it was so. God called the
dry ground "land," and the gathered waters he called "seas."
And God saw that it was good.

Then God said, "Let the land produce vegetation:
seed-bearing plants and trees on the land that bear fruit
with seed in it, according to their various kinds."
And it was so. The land produced vegetation: plants bearing
seed according to their kinds and trees bearing fruit with seed in
it according to their kinds. And God saw that it was good.
And there was evening, and there was morning—the third day.

And God said, "Let there be lights in the expanse of the sky to separate the day from the night, and let them serve as signs to mark seasons and days and years, and let them be lights in the expanse of the sky to give light on the earth." And it was so.

God made two great lights—the greater light to govern the day and the lesser light to govern the night. He also made the stars.

God set them in the expanse of the sky to give light on the earth,
to govern the day and the night, and to separate light from darkness.
And God saw that it was good.
And there was evening, and there was morning—the fourth day.

And God said, "Let the water teem with living creatures,

and let birds fly above the earth across the expanse of the sky."

So God created the great creatures of the sea and every living and
moving thing with which the water teems, according to their kinds,
and every winged bird according to its kind. And God saw that it was good.

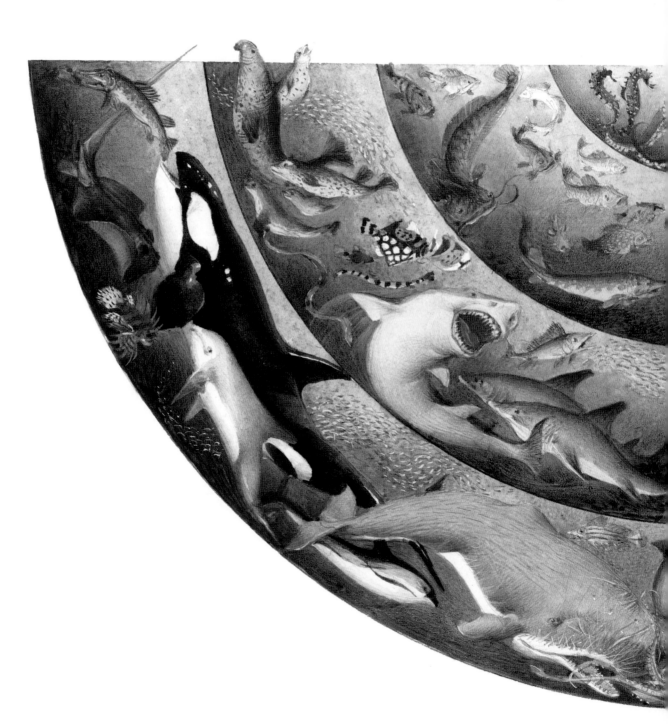

God blessed them and said, "Be fruitful and increase in number and
fill the water in the seas, and let the birds increase on the earth."
And there was evening, and there was morning—the fifth day.

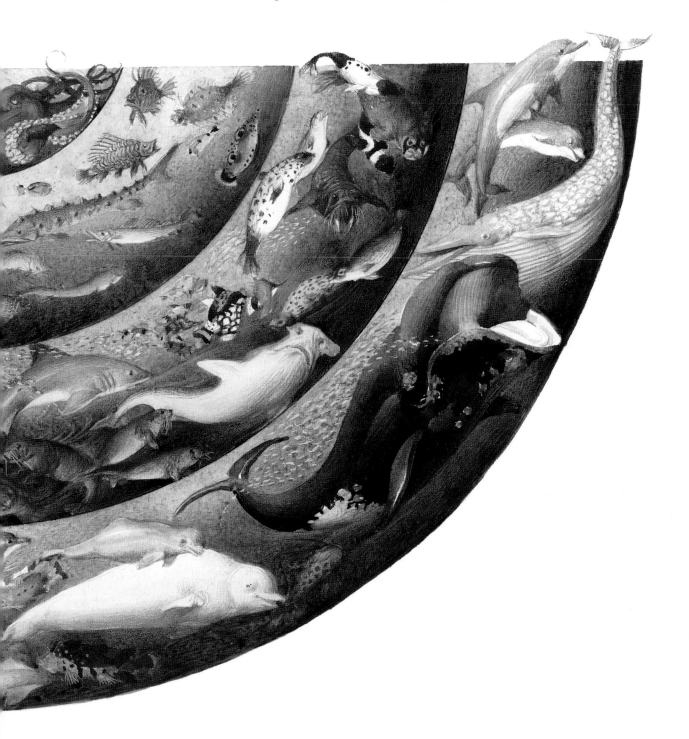

And God said, "Let the land produce living creatures according to
their kinds: livestock, creatures that move along the ground,
and wild animals, each according to its kind." And it was so.

God made the wild animals according to their kinds, the livestock
according to their kinds, and all the creatures that move
along the ground according to their kinds. And God saw that it was good.

Then God said, "Let us make man in our image, in our likeness, and let them rule over the fish of the sea and the birds of the air, over the livestock, over all the earth, and over all the creatures that move along the ground."

So God created man in his own image, in the image of God he created him; male and female he created them.

God blessed them and said to them, "Be fruitful and increase in number; fill the earth and subdue it. Rule over the fish of the sea and the birds of the air and over every living creature that moves on the ground."

Then God said, "I give you every seed-bearing plant on the face of the whole earth and every tree that has fruit with seed in it. They will be yours for food.

And to all the beasts of the earth and all the birds of the air and all the creatures that move on the ground— everything that has the breath of life in it—I give every green plant for food." And it was so.

God saw all that he had made, and it was very good. And there was evening, and there was morning—the sixth day.

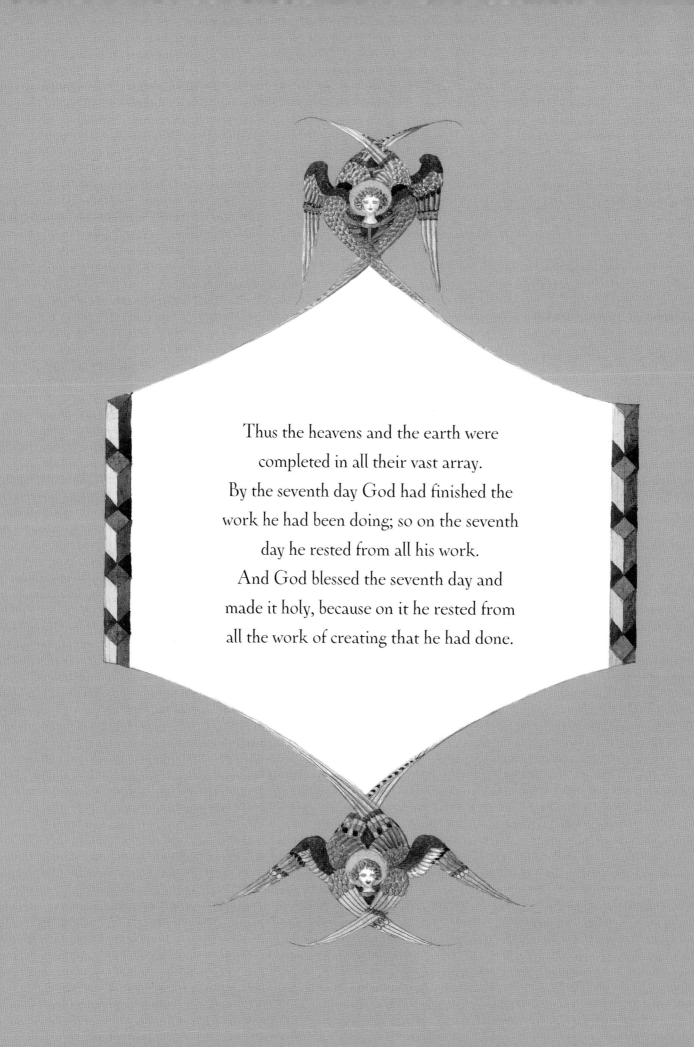

Thus the heavens and the earth were
completed in all their vast array.
By the seventh day God had finished the
work he had been doing; so on the seventh
day he rested from all his work.
And God blessed the seventh day and
made it holy, because on it he rested from
all the work of creating that he had done.

Dear Reader,

The words of this book come directly from the Bible. When we think about the Bible, we think of it as a book. It has two covers and a certain set of stories within it. Of course it's a special book. One of the truly special things about it is that these stories didn't stop happening when the books of the Bible were collected in the form we know today. God kept working in his creation from that time even until today.

If you could trace all the people in the Bible through their descendents right up until today you would find that these people are your ancestors, no matter where you live or what culture you belong to. The stories and words of the Bible are not just any old stories, they are OUR stories—the words of our spiritual ancestors. What you hold in your hands is not just a picture book of ancient words, it is part of your story, and thus part of you.

So while we hope you enjoy this book, our goal is really that you will hear these words as words spoken to you from a distant relative, as meaningful today as they were the day they were written.

Sincerely,

Zondervan

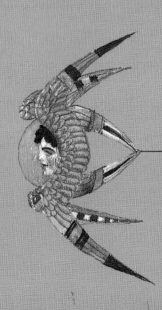